Butterfly

Ian Rowlands was born in the Rhondda Valley. He trained as an actor before turning to writing and directing in the early 1990s. His full length plays for Theatr y Byd include: *The Sin Eaters*, *Glissando on an Empty Harp*, *Love in Plastic* (performed within an installation by Tim Davies), *Marriage of Convenience*, *Blue Heron in the Womb*, *New South Wales* and *Pacific*. His TV credits include *A Light in the Valley* (winner of a Royal Television Society award) and *Blink* for the BBC, based upon the full-length play of that name. He is currently Artistic Director of Llwyfan Gogledd Cymru having previously been the Artistic Director of Cwmni Theatr Gwynedd, Bara Caws and Theatr y Byd.

Ian lives in Carmarthen, works in Caernarfon and dreams of an integrated transport policy for Wales!

Butterfly

Ian Rowlands

PARTHIAN

Parthian
The Old Surgery
Napier Street
Cardigan
SA43 1ED

www.parthianbooks.co.uk

First published in 2006
© Ian Rowlands 2006
All Rights Reserved

ISBN 1 902638 96 4
      9 781902 638966

Cover design by Lucy Llewellyn
Cover photograph by Tim Davies
Inner design by www.lloydrobson.com
Printed and bound by Dinefwr Press, Llandybïe, Wales

Published with the financial support of the Welsh
Books Council

British Library Cataloguing in Publication Data –
A cataloguing record for this book is available from the
British Library

Butterfly

Butterfly was commissioned and produced by Theatr Y Byd with the support of the Arts Council of Wales. First presented at The Riverfront Arts Centre, Newport on St David's Day 2006, and then on tour throughout Wales.

The play was performed within an installation by Tim Davies. Original song 'Butterfly' written and performed by Amy Wadge.

Cast:

Man	–	Ian Saynor
Boy	–	Sam Miller
Butterfly	–	Alison John

Creative Team:

Director	–	Chris Morgan
Lighting Designer	–	Dave Roxburgh
Costume	–	Allie Saunders
Company Stage Manager	–	Emily Cooper
Technical Stage Manager	–	Duncan Thompson
Technical Assistant to Tim Davies	–	Andrew Hamley
Administrator	–	Stephen Burkitt-Harrington
Press and Marketing	–	Anne Keeling

'With mirth and laughter let old wrinkles come, and let my liver rather heat with wine, than my heart cool with mortifying groans.'
                           – Gratiano (Merchant of Venice)

Scene One – The Pick up

In the room of dead butterflies.

MAN: Welcome to my life.

BOY: Thanks. (*He hovers at the entrance.*)

MAN: Don't stand on ceremony...

BOY: Sorry?

MAN: Take a seat.

There are no seats to sit on.

MAN: Would you like a drink?

BOY: Mmm?

MAN: Do you imbibe, Reverend?

BOY: Do I what?

MAN: Wine?

BOY : Sure. Don't like sweet shit though.

MAN: Not sweet, certainly not shit; Montrachet.

BOY: As long as it's wet.

MAN: Van Gogh, lost on the blind.

BOY: What!

MAN: Only the best for a guest!

BOY : Thanks.

Pause.

MAN: Can't place the accent. Where are you from?

BOY: Around and about.

MAN: Student?

BOY: Ex.

MAN: Up for work?

BOY: Searching.

MAN: Aren't we all...

BOY : But I think I've found something...

MAN: Well let's drink to that, whatever that is.

BOY looks uncertain.

MAN: Don't be scared; no lizards in my wine. Drink and be merry, for tomorrow we die.

BOY: Cheers!

MAN: Bottoms up.

Silence.

MAN: So tell me, in all honesty, what did you really think of tonight's exhibition?

BOY : It was...

His hesitancy is taken as criticism.

MAN: Exactly. As if we haven't seen two women sew their nipples together before; and with perter breasts! Eh?

BOY: Well...

MAN: If I have to endure one more *confessio* from a mediocre talent, I swear I'll torch both the artist and the work. Do you know what I dream of?

BOY: No.

MAN: I dream of carrying acid in a pen, so that when I get really angry, I can just squirt and destroy; like a tube bomber; instant fucking critic.

BOY: Sure...

MAN: Not that I'm the violent type, but the mundane eats me, especially when I have to read the shit artists write to justify themselves. It's an insult to literacy. Artists should be banned from writing anything. Parliament should pass an act and save us all from their anal prose! Anal probe, that's what's bloody needed! 60,000 volts! Create that, you talentless bastards! I am bored by the shock tactics of the obese.

BOY: Sorry?

MAN: Art 'nour days is 'Grosz'; lardy and desperate, a fat-arsed Louisiana woman who's lost sight of her feet. They're down there somewhere, but God knows where?

Beat.

MAN: You see, all artists, in essence, are searching for their big statement, when in the end, there is only one question. 'How do we make sense of life in a godless world?' To which there is no answer, no statement to be made! If the most brilliant minds of all generations are stumped by it, what hope have the vast majority of visionless artists got, who think it's *de rigueur* to shave Malevich's square in their pubes. I mean we all saw that in Venice!

BOY: Did we?

MAN: Well some of us did! I think that we've come to the point that if anyone even thinks they have an artistic bent they should first be tortured to ascertain their potential ability, and if found wanting, they should be forced to work in a salmon wanking factory for the rest of their lives; save us all from their future dross!

Believe me, it's only a matter of time before some desperate artist superglues a cock up a crack in an attempt to be original. Saying that, some fool probably has; in bloody Wales or somewhere where imagination is gossamer thin! There is little original thought in this world, only sensation! Fuck art! Not that I'm championing craft. God forbid, any one who champions craft above art is artistically dead that's a *sine qua non*. I am bored with the desperate. Bored rigid by the fucking wretched.... Discuss in ten thousand words!

BOY: You've lost me.

6

MAN: Art! Think about it.

BOY: I've never thought about it.

MAN: Then think about it now... be a foil to my rhetoric.

BOY: I don't know.

MAN: You don't need to know, just have an opinion, I can't fuck anything without an opinion.

BOY: I'm sorry.

MAN: Give me your opinion. 'In my opinion, art is...'

BOY: It's sort of... over there...

MAN: Over where?

BOY: Over there...

MAN: Why?

BOY: It's never... never touched me...

MAN: Then you're the lucky one and I'm Bessie bastard Bighead; kissed once, but never again.

BOY: You've lost me.

Pause.

MAN: Arsenal are doing well this season aren't they!

BOY: I don't know, I hate football.

7

MAN: Oh...

Pause.

BOY: Can I ask you a question, mate?

MAN: Of course. As long as the answer's compromising.

BOY: It might be.

MAN: Good.

BOY: Don't think me rude.

MAN: Oh, please let me.

BOY: Why all the butterflies?

MAN: Butterflies!

Pause.

BOY: Yeah, all the butterflies...

MAN: And moths...

BOY: And moths.

MAN: Don't mistake butterflies for moths.

BOY: Same sort of thing.

MAN: God no; one flies to the flame, the other flies in grace.

BOY: What?

MAN: *Muchos muchos* fucking different, *amigo*.

BOY: If you say so.

MAN: Don't take my word, look.

BOY: What am I looking for?

MAN: Scorch marks, and clubbed antennae.

BOY: What?

MAN: Butterflies have clubbed antennae, moths have not.

BOY: Is that a fact?

MAN: You tell me, I've never looked.

BOY (*he looks*): My mother says a butterfly was trapped in the room when she was born. 'Flying things' freak her. Took her to a butterfly park one day. Thought it'd be therapeutic. All the little kids were loving it, but she went ape; killed some really rare ones. She'd torch this place given half a chance.

MAN: And you?

BOY: I like it.

MAN: Why?

BOY: It's sort of... not what I expected...

MAN: And what did you expect?

BOY: Well, you said you were an art collector...

MAN: And critic.

BOY: And critic, yeah, so I thought your walls would be full of art and shit.

MAN: And shit!

BOY: Just more of it.

MAN: You presumed.

BOY: Suppose...

MAN: Presumption is Semtex.

BOY: What?

MAN: Blows reason apart.

BOY: No offence.

MAN: I am bloody offended.

BOY: Sorry.

MAN: You should supplicate, kiss my feet... later perhaps. To be honest, you're not wholly wrong. Up until a few years ago, you couldn't see the wall for the canvas; hundreds of souls stolen for a song from artists who should've known better than to give away so much of themselves, so cheaply. But, these days, as you can see, I prefer dead 'flying things'.

10

BOY: Interesting...

MAN: I'm sorry?

BOY: Interesting.

MAN: Now that is a word to kill hospitality dead. Interesting. I should throw you out of the door just for uttering it. Surely you can do better than 'interesting'!

BOY: A bit crazy perhaps... idiosyncratic?

MAN: Now there's a word to conjure with, idiosyncratic!

BOY: Is that interesting enough?

MAN: Deserving of every sip of Burgundian sun. More wine?

BOY : Wouldn't say no. (*He selects a butterfly.*) So what's this one called?

MAN: That one? That's 'Bathroom, July 23rd'.

BOY: Sorry?

MAN: 'Bathroom, July 23rd.'

BOY: No, its name.

MAN: That is its name. My home, my sodding classification.

BOY : Sure. What about this one?

MAN: That one there, if it's ok by you, is called 'Kitchen, August 25th'.

BOY: And that one?

MAN: 'Hall, June 14th'.

BOY: And this one?

MAN: Bedroom, May 7th.

BOY: Why?

MAN: Why May the 7th?

BOY: No. Why the whole date thing?

MAN: It's where they died and when. Their deaths being their defining moments, not their names in bloody Latin. Little fragments of being, anonymous tragedies frozen in grace. Look at them... closer still. Aren't they exquisite? How can any art compare with them? Eh? How can mediocrity touch the divine? They are more poignant than any painting, don't you think; better executed than any conception?

BOY: I don't know.

MAN: You never want to know, take my word for it.

Pause.

BOY: So, where are all your paintings then, if you got rid of them?

MAN: Buried. Certain fathoms deep!

BOY: You chucked them!

MAN: God no! I'm idiosyncratic not stupid. They're in storage.

BOY: Why?

MAN: It's a long story.

BOY: Please...

MAN: I tell no one, sorry.

BOY: I'm a no-one, you can tell me.

MAN: And, if I do, what will my reward be?

BOY: We'll see.

MAN: We will, will we? An acquaintance of mine once took a flighty young thing into his confidence, a pretty young thing like you. The pretty young thing handcuffed him naked to the stove. Three days later my acquaintance was found by his cleaner; the wages of sin are death by embarrassment.

BOY: I won't embarrass you.

MAN: Compromise, but never embarrass. Promise?

BOY: Promise. So, tell me.

MAN (*he considers*): For audacity, I will.... At one time, art, to me, was the passion of a myriad Christs brave enough to hang upon walls for all our sins; the apotheosis of being. From Slade and Goldsmiths they came! I worshipped them, and craved their brilliance. And over the years, I amassed a sizable collection; mostly British, post-1950. They were kind to me; never bite the hand that feeds, I guess! Kitaj hung above the mantle piece, Hodgkin was my window, Auerbach, Riley, Bacon melting in the kitchen, a 'Naked Shit' in my toilet courtesy of G 'n' G! And in the salty air of my bedroom, a Hockney! And then, the new generation of young 'Turks' graced me with their gifts. I was one lucky-bugger critic! But overnight... things changed....

BOY: How?

MAN (*laughs to himself*): How? Do you know why I became a critic?

BOY: Why?

MAN: Failure. I had no talent as an artist. God, I can barely paint a wall and the nearest I ever got to sculpture was IKEA – assembled a wardrobe for a friend once, it ended up like a piece of bloody Irish public art; the bastard love child of Billy bookcase and Anthony fucking Caro! Mine was a case of those who can, do; those who can't, criticise! Bitching always came naturally to me; it's my Oxford cynicism.

BOY: You went to Oxford?

MAN: Of course. There I learnt to bitch and envy with the best of them. And it was there, I began desiring the souls of gods; a corrosive passion, it ate me... *aqua fortis* to the heart no Zantac can cure! Do you have a burning passion?

BOY: Me?

MAN: Is there another in this room!

14

BOY: Nothing.

MAN: You must have a desire? What seduces you, what grabs you by the balls and says, live?

BOY: Things...

MAN: Specific things?

BOY: Just things.

MAN: What things?

BOY: Some things.

MAN: Some things?

BOY: Sort of thing.

MAN: You're either enigmatic or bloody stupid!

BOY: I've got a degree.

MAN: Where from?

BOY: Bradford.

MAN: What for? Eating curry?

BOY: Conflict Resolution. It's how I tolerate your crap without hitting you.

MAN: Aw, that hurt. Very good, though; very good. Bradford, eh!

BOY: To be honest, it was the only place I could get in.

MAN: Well, well, an honest CV!

BOY: No point lying.

MAN: No. Honesty's a rare quality these days, it should be rewarded. As we're trading honesties, and in a spirit of reconciliation, my confession is, yes, I went up to Oxford, however, the truth is, I went to Oxford Poly. But I keep my past on a need-to-know basis, only. I trust that you'll never tell.

BOY: I don't know anyone who would give a shit.

MAN: Don't be cruel... someone might.

Pause.

MAN: So you have no vocation in life?

BOY: No.

MAN: Must be freeing... maybe not. I had little choice. At fourteen, I was fucked by Egon Schiele just when I was looking for an awakening.

BOY: Had a postcard of his once.

MAN: Schiele's!

BOY: Yes!

MAN: Common ground at last!

16

BOY: Mother and child thing.

MAN: Yes, yes...

BOY: Quite nice.

MAN: Nice! And, let me guess, was it also interesting? Your words are concrete boots, dragging the sublime down to the bed of the Danube! Shiele was not fucking interesting, like a sodding Vettriano painting! He burned! His work was aflame with ambiguity and passion; a ferocious incandescence; his heart was potassium! Standing before his self-portrait masturbating defined the rest of my life. From that moment on, there was only one path for me; a life of beauty, endless bitching and appropriation. At least I didn't sell insurance! Is there any more wine left?

BOY: A drop.

MAN: If you'd oblige...

BOY: And the butterfly thing?

MAN: Patience, my little moth.

BOY: My name is...

MAN: 'Little moth', to me. I am a critic. I make and break careers with the stroke of my pen. I lived surrounded by shards of artists' souls hanging upon the walls of my personal Uffizi.

However, one day... there's always one day, isn't there? One day, I happened to open the paper at the obituaries and saw that a very promising artist I'd once known had died; twenty-seven, a tragedy. Under that canvas lies her soul. Bought it for a song before she was discovered... by me of course! I loaned that painting to a museum. I hadn't seen the artist for five years; lost touch with her when she left London... not a word.

And so when I read about her death, I immediately phoned to ask where my painting was. 'Oh, it's not here,' they said. 'We thought you knew.' 'Knew what?' 'Knew she took it, about a year ago'. 'I beg your fucking pardon,' I said 'She said she had your permission.' 'But I knew nothing of this.' 'Oh...' they said. 'So where is it now? I asked, and they said they didn't know. So I slammed down the phone.... I was fuming.

She had the cheek to steal my painting! It's irrelevant whether she painted it or not, it was my property. She's signed the bloody receipt, for God's sake. It was my possession. I owned it! She had no right to pilfer it like a Chav, after all I'd done for her!

So there I was, wishing holy hell upon her, when the phone rang, and it was her partner, Bill. I'd never met... Bill, but I hated him. His name always sounded like an invoice! 'So sorry to hear,' I said. 'Thanks' he said and 'Would you loan the painting for the funeral?' 'Of course... and where is the painting now?' 'It's with me,' he said. 'Oh! And where's me?' 'In Chester,' and before I could ask why, he came straight out with 'and would you like to sell it?'

Would I like to sell it! Indecent shit! To broach such a delicate subject when she'd only just died! Husband or not! Twat! Calm, I thought, calm. 'I would prefer not to discuss the matter at such an upsetting time.' 'Of course,' he said, his voice trailing off. 'I'll see you at the funeral then'.

The church was crammed; too many people to recognise anyone. Telegrams from dying RA's, bad family poems! A young death always brings out the worst, doesn't it!

After my chat with Bill, I expected a retrospective, there was only one painting on show – mine. The first time I'd seen Butterfly for five years.

BOY: Butterfly?

MAN: Yes. It was like staring at a distant shag across a crowded opening.

The sermon sucked the life out of me, waste of bloody breath! I kept my attention glued to the canvas not the cross! That solitary canvas; a female Christ in a male church of sub-Tintoretto shit.

After the service, and the congregation had dispersed, I crept back into the empty church and stood before my Butterfly. She seemed sad to see me. I begged her forgiveness, but there was no acceptance. I knew she didn't want me there. And for one brief moment, I considered parting company with her. Bill's need was probably greater than mine....

BOY: Would you do it now?

MAN: Return Butterfly to her husband?

BOY: Yes.

MAN: God no! It was a brief moment of sentimentality, it soon passed. An old woman stood next to me; all Yardley and blue rinse. 'Such a waste of talent, makes you question is there a God, doesn't it?' she said. 'And did you know, she was nominated for a Jerwood!' Of course I fucking knew, I nominated her. 'Such a wonderful painting, isn't it?' 'Yes' I spat, 'and I own it!' I own it....

Pause.

19

MAN: Luckily, the old woman hadn't heard what I said. She muttered something and left us alone again; two souls stranded on the raft of the bastard Medusa! What did I own? Not just a piece of art, but a splinter of soul; a canvas, so important to the artist, that she re-appropriated it before she died! What could I ever own? Nothing! In that church, I shattered like Dalí's head... to be honest, I've yet to pick up all the pieces.

So when I got home that night, I took each painting I possessed down from my walls and bubble-wrapped it. Next day I arranged storage for the lot.

BOY: Why?

MAN: Because I felt.... Perhaps I should've sold insurance after all, eh?

BOY: Yeah....

MAN: God forbid! A few weeks after that, I received a phone call from Bill. Would I like to sell the painting now? 'No' I said. Then, would I loan it for a series of exhibitions?' Obscure galleries, small towns. 'Of course'. Over the following months, one exhibition turned into another, there were excuses but I let them ride, I was too ashamed to bargain.

Anyway, a year or so after the funeral, Bill phoned me again. There was to be an exhibition in a cafe in Croydon – what a place to die – a cafe in bloody Croydon! Anyway, after that, the painting would be returned to me. There was no more talk of purchase, thank God. Some weeks later, he sent Butterfly around by courier, too busy to come in person. I helped carry the painting up from the street, tipped Dan the Van twenty pounds and was left, alone with her.

She hated me. I could sense it. So I covered her Titian gaze and no one, no one, apart from me, has seen my Butterfly from that day to this. She flies in grace for me, and me alone.

BOY: I see.

MAN: Rape me, do whatever you want with me. But do not... do not ask to look at that painting. It's my Bluebeard's door and my blade is keen. Understand?

BOY: Sure

MAN: Apart from that, everything else in my life is yours, take it, use it, please God, abuse it. Mmm? So... does truth deserve a kiss?

BOY: Maybe...

MAN approaches BOY and begins to kiss him, first upon the lips, then his neck, whilst going for his crotch with his hand.

BOY (*thinking*): *Oh, fuck... fuck off... just fuck off... please fuck off.*

MAN (*pausing, sensing something is wrong*): Am I going too fast?

BOY: I'd better be going.

MAN: Did I do something wrong?

BOY: No, it's just I'm too far gone.

MAN: Sleep here.

BOY: Not tonight.

MAN: I'll sleep out here, you take my bed.

BOY: I need some air.

MAN: It's April out there!

BOY: I'm fucked.

MAN: Stay....

BOY: I can't.

MAN: If I paid you, would it make a difference?

BOY: What?

MAN: If I paid you, you wouldn't have to touch me, just sleep here....

BOY: You're joking.

MAN: Not even with me.

BOY: Don't...

MAN: No?

BOY: Fuck off!

MAN: Just company.

BOY: What the fuck do you think I am?

MAN: I don't know what you are.

BOY: Presumption, my fuck!

MAN: Ok, I'm sorry... my mistake....

BOY: Damn right!

Pause.

MAN: Look, let's be Japanese about this. Whatever's said in cups...

BOY: You are one sick shit!

MAN: But, I've bared my soul to you.

BOY: Your choice.

MAN: You asked.

BOY: So?

MAN: Look, take my number, just in case.

BOY: I know where you live.

MAN: The City's a big place.

BOY: I'll remember if I need to.

MAN: Hope you do.

BOY: Don't hold your breath.

MAN: At least you didn't handcuff me!

Beat.

BOY: Thanks for the wine.

MAN: My pleasure.

BOY: I prefer red.

MAN: Next time....

BOY goes to exit.

MAN: Call me.

A female singing voice is heard. It is a distant sound.

MAN: Please? Please, Little Moth...

BOY (*looks, with stabbing eyes*): Don't beg, it's ugly past forty! (*He exits the flat.*)

MAN: Bastard.... Bastard!

Scene Two – The Seduction

As BUTTERFLY sings, MAN approaches the canvas. He reveals a painting/work of art entitled Self-Portrait as Butterfly. The central figure is missing from the image.

MAN: Oh, my Butterfly. I guess it's just you and me again, the two of us. No triangle of intrigue for us tonight, just a simple one-on-one; butterfly and collector; love, net and a killing jar.

Perhaps you're wondering who he was, boy with the Mapplethorpe arse? Who he? We know not. But what? He was beyond imagination, that's what; an incubus in the night, sin made flesh. Little shit! I'd burn all my years for one dance from that little moth around my dying flame. I could see you dance for him. Slut! Dance for me. Dance in grace, my darling. Not tonight? Never tonight....

I remember the first time I saw you, cocooned in a quilted coat. I followed you across the Millennium Bridge into County Hall, then watched as you cracked your cocoon in the cloak room and flew around the gallery as if Saatchi had just bought your leaver's show and you were wondering where it would be hung; which he did, which it never was! Past Sid Vicious and the elephant shit you flitted gracefully amongst the Sensations until you alighted in front of butterflies on a canvas by Hirst. I loathe that painting; hate the series. It was my concept! Ever since I was a child I've had a passion for specimen cases; frozen eternities, gas chamber beauties. I loved dead butterflies years before Hirst was born. He stole my one stab at original thought, the bastard! Conceptual theft, pure and simple, the acid in my pen boiled.

But you stood before Butterflies in yellow, took a sketch book out of your bag, and drew clean confident lines; graphite on white. I watched transfixed as your hands, delicate and Georgian, drew life into being. And saw, there, above your wrist, a tattoo. At some point, a butterfly had landed upon your skin and you had absorbed it. In that gallery, I fought the urge to scalpel that butterfly off your wrist and pin it bloody to my heart.

There is a cough at the door. MAN covers the painting, in haste.

BOY: The door was open.

MAN: You didn't close it?

BOY: I left quickly.

MAN: Indecent haste!

BOY: I'm sorry.

MAN: What did you see?

BOY: Nothing.

MAN: What did you hear?

BOY: Nothing.

MAN: Nothing?

BOY: No.

Pause.

MAN: Then you're doubly welcome.

Beat.

BOY: About earlier.

MAN: Sh...

BOY: I want to apologise.

MAN: Don't. You'll just make things worse.

BOY: I didn't mean to hurt you.

MAN: God help if you ever do.

BOY: I came back to say I'm sorry.

MAN: Forty is the new bloody grey!

BOY: Don't you mean black?

MAN: I know what I mean! I have all my own teeth! And they can bite!

BOY: I'm sorry, It's just... it's just... well, to be honest, I've never, you know... I've never... been, in this sort of situation before... and it scared me.

MAN: And what sort of situation is this?

BOY: I've never been...

MAN: To Paris in the rain?

BOY: With a man. I've never been with a man before.

MAN: Oh! A v...

BOY: Please don't say a virgin!

MAN: A very interesting situation.

BOY: Interesting?

MAN: Each word has its time and place!

Pause.

BOY: I just felt vulnerable, that's all. I've never been with a man with quite this intention before.

MAN: I have no intention.

BOY: You had.

MAN: I thought it was mutual intent.

BOY: It was.

MAN: You picked me up. Let's not forget that.

BOY: I know. I just couldn't handle it; all sorts of stuff going on, my mind was racing. I just had to get out.

Beat.

MAN: Is it truly your first time?

BOY: Yes.

Pause.

MAN: I see. Well, don't be scared.

BOY: I am.

MAN: We've all been there.

BOY: It feels odd, that's all.

MAN: Wrong?

BOY: Wrong... but right.

MAN: Yes.

BOY: Strange.

MAN: Different?

BOY: Just odd; your stubble on my neck... and the smell of your sweat...

MAN: Am I high?

BOY: No, just not what I'm used to. I'm used to women... and they smell like... a clean bed, you know?

MAN: They can do.

BOY: But you smell...

MAN: Like a tramp's cheese?

BOY: Like a challenge.

MAN: Oh... is that good, bad or ugly?

BOY: Just an impression.

MAN: I can smell like a clean bed if you want me to.

BOY: No, a challenge is fine.

MAN: Good.

BOY: It'll just take time. I want to be here. I didn't make a mistake. I made the 'B' line for you, you're right... I just find it difficult.

Pause.

MAN: I understand. Believe me.

BOY: Yeah.

MAN: No, I do. I was sixteen when I was you. I caught the bus to London without my parents knowing. Petrified, just like you. I didn't know what was going to happen, only knew that it would. I got off the bus at Victoria and headed straight for Heaven, the only place I knew of. It was frightening... but freeing at the same time; the mirrored *pissoir* thrilled me, school showers with knobs on; everybody looking. I was picked up by an actor who'd appeared in some Seventies landmark gay film. He took me back to his flat and that night, I guess, was a night like this. You are me; your fears were mine. He was gentle, I owe you that. So, I'm sorry I came on a bit quick. Believe me, I had no intention of abusing you. These days I tend only to abuse myself. I was just... presumptuous, I guess.

BOY: It's ok.

Pause.

MAN: Let's start again, blank canvas....

BOY: Yeah....

MAN: I have a bottle of Cristal I've been saving for such an occasion. (*He stops.*) Damn, it's white... sparkling though!

BOY: Sparkling's good.

MAN: A celebration.... (*He goes for the wine.*) So I am a challenge, am I?

BOY: Well...

MAN: And yet you came back.

BOY: I never quit.

MAN: I'm glad.

BOY: I didn't want to quit... just fear.

MAN: It's natural. You know, an old theatre luvvie once told me that what actors don't realise is, in auditions, the director is usually more nervous than them. The actors think they harbour all the fear, but it's not true.

BOY: No?

MAN: No. The more we have to lose, the more we fear. You thought I was steel?

BOY: You seemed cool.

MAN: Cool enough to drivel on! Do you think I would drivel on if I was calm, do you? It's been a long, long time since I was last in this situation. I feel as vulnerable as you... doubly so. I fear the ridicule of youth; its rejection. I think we both need a touch more Dutch courage tonight?

BOY: Sure.

Pause.

MAN: So, why did you pick me? I'm Billtong and you're fresh meat.

BOY: What?

MAN: I'm rancid, you're perfumed. I have white pubes for God's sake!

BOY: White pubes!

MAN: The door is still open, I presume.

BOY: You're joking?

MAN: Life is hardly *une plaisanterie*, my friend. It's an evil joke at the expense of the living. The sort of joke that rises out of abject fear; two female suicide bombers trying rucksacks in a camping store, 'does my bomb look big in this?' It's fucking sick. You don't want me. If I were you, I'd make tracks a second time before you discover how corrupt flesh can become. You don't want to know that yet, not when beauty becomes you so well, my bittersweet Vanitas...

BOY: What?

MAN (*breaking his reverie*): 'Champaigne!' (*He pops the cork.*)

BOY: Great. But I chose to come back, I didn't have to.

MAN: No.

Beat.

32

MAN: Why?

BOY: Does it matter?

MAN: It matters to me. Tell me why.

BOY: I don't know.

MAN: Please....

Glasses of wine are poured.

BUTTERFLY sings under italicised thoughts:

BOY: *Should I tell you a truth; an Electra truth, how I always loved my father nude after a bath? The desire I felt to touch his sex bigger than a child's hand.*

MAN: *Lie to me, Little Moth.*

BOY: *How a teacher blew me off in his front room. 'You must experience everything if you are to grow' he said; the fuck-up of pleasure and shame.*

MAN: *Lie and there's hope.*

BOY: *How we used to wank over a five-P; my friends'd wank for Tracy, but I'd wank for them.*

MAN: *Lie, my moth, truth bores itself to death!*

BOY: I just felt the need to.

MAN: Desire?

BOY: I guess.

MAN: Then, desire's good enough for me.

MAN hands BOY a glass of wine.

BOY: Thanks.

MAN (*offering a toast*): To desire, and bugger Buddha!

They drink.

BOY: Sorry?

MAN: Denial of desire is the root of all suffering! *N'est pas?*

BOY: If you say so.

MAN: Oh, it is, I learnt the hard way. When I was a student I saw a small painting by Lowry. It would've cost me a whole term's grant, which would hardly have made life Franciscan, but living would've been a pinch. I desired that painting... desired it with my whole being. But, in the end, I dithered over several pints in the Students Union and didn't buy it. And I regret my indecision to this day. I hesitated and lost; a collector's tale; a fisherman's, but not as fishy!

I should've acted upon my desire. Butterfly, on the other hand, desired and took without a second thought... impulsive! Dream, action; action, dream, no distinction for her. She was beautiful, wild with dreaming... you would've liked her... and she, you...

BOY: Sure.

MAN: She spent a whole term's grant on a small sketch by Gwen John; braver than me, but then I never had an older me to keep me, did I! She brought it home and presented it for approval, like a child bearing treasure from a forgotten field or a friend who once drove a hundred miles to the Arnolfini to buy a pair of Tracy Emin's knickers! 'And scratch 'n' sniff,' he said!

But something niggled me about the drawing. Gwen John rarely signed and the pencil strokes didn't seem light enough. But I said nothing. I let Butterfly believe she owned the essence of beauty.

Then one evening we argued; nothing important, she was late for a gallery opening, she smelled of sex. Bitch! So I ope'd my lips, 'Your Gwen John's a fake! If you don't believe me, get a second opinion!' She was stunned; knew I wouldn't lie about such things, provenance is sacred, *terroir*! I didn't have to say 'I told you so' when I was proved right, but I did. And I hate myself for that... for destroying her dream.

BOY: Cruel.

MAN: I just hope I won't destroy yours.

BOY: You're not my dream.

MAN (*deflated*): Oh....

BOY: I don't mean that in an awful way.

MAN: In which way do you mean it?

BOY: My dream is... in me.

MAN: As all dreams are.

BOY: Yeah, but it's not a future dream, I've already lived it.

MAN: A ready-made!

BOY: More memory than dream, really. But I didn't live it entirely, so the dream is still fantasy, if you know what I mean?

MAN: Now you've lost me.

BOY (*thinks, then*): It's hard to explain.

MAN: Please.

Beat.

BOY: I was married at twenty, right.

MAN: Sounds like a bloody nightmare to me.

BOY: Yeah, but it's what was expected of me. It happened before I realised it. I remember sitting in my girlfriend's parents' house one evening. 'We hear that Debbie's been sleeping with you in Bradford,' her father said, as if it was a big deal. Shit, we'd been at it since before she was legal. 'Well, we think it's only right that you make a decent woman of her when you finish your degree. Don't you?' And he was a big man, fists like hammers, I didn't dare say no. I don't even know if she really wanted to marry me either, but her dad was a bastard, so we did. To be honest, for me, it was mostly just guilt.

MAN: Guilt?

BOY: Yeah. (*It is difficult for him to relate.*)Because... well, a few months before that... something happened.

MAN: One of your things.

BOY: Yeah.

MAN: A salacious thing?

BOY: I guess.

MAN: Oh good.

Beat.

BOY: It's difficult to...

Beat.

BOY: What happened was... well, a few months before the 'chat', I went to Liverpool – a work thing. Debbie'd arranged for me to stay with her brother. He was in Uni there. So that night we went for a Chinese, eat all you can for six quid, then on to the pub. And we were laughing and all shy like boys shouldn't be, or not like I thought I would ever be... all coy like a girl, you know?

MAN: 'Had we but world enough and time...'

BOY (*thrown*): Sorry?

MAN: I'm dreaming with you, please continue.

BOY (*disconcerted, but continues*): Anyway, after a few pints, we went back to his room for some wine and a DVD.

Turned in about three. I was whacked, but I lay awake on the lilo at the bottom of his bed for ages, I couldn't sleep. I just lay on my back, couldn't lay on my stomach I ached so much. I was hyper aware of every sound; the smallest rustle, lightest breath. I felt electric; all up for it, but nervous as fuck.

I shouldn't have been feeling such things. Not just the fact that he was a man, but because he was my girlfriend's brother, you know. It piled guilt on guilt. In the end, I couldn't stand it any more, so I went to the bathroom to sort myself out so that I could get to sleep. And I was about to come, when he walked in, 'I thought you were being sick,' he said, and I shot into my hand in front of him. He knew I wasn't thinking about Debbie at that moment. He just smiled and closed the door. Nothing was said, and I just crawled back into my sleeping bag. Next day I left before breakfast, I couldn't face him.

From then on, when I made love to Debbie, I saw her brother in her face. Five years of seeing him in her, sitting next to him at family get-togethers, back-slapping, shaking hands, wanting to shake his cock! In the end I thought, 'Fuck this, I need to sort a few things out', so I got out and left for London. Not that I think I'm *gay* gay though, just... just questions, you know?

MAN: Of course.

BOY: Since being here, I've just looked for work and kept my head down. I did check out the gay bars in City Limits but never got it together to visit them. Then I met an old school friend in Stockwell. We went out a few times, just a couple of pints, and he sort of guessed a few things about me. So, a week or so ago, he asked whether I'd want to go to an exhibition. 'You never know,' he said, 'all sorts'll be there.' Well, I'd never been to an opening before so I said,

'Art's not my thing'. 'You don't have to like art', he said, 'it's just a piss-up'. And I thought, ok, what the hell.

MAN: What the hell.

BOY: Not that I haven't seen paintings before, it's just that I haven't looked at them, if you know what I mean!

MAN: They're 'over there'!

BOY: Yeah, especially conceptual shit like tonight...

MAN: Shit? An opinion, at last!

BOY: I didn't mean shit like that, sorry.

MAN: Don't be sorry.

BOY: To be honest, I wouldn't know shit from shit. My mother, though, she would've had a few things to say about the sewing; stitching could have been neater!

MAN: That was their statement.

BOY: And the video was a bit amateur, wasn't it?

MAN: That was their intent.

BOY: All out of focus.

MAN: Impressionistic.

BOY: Didn't impress me, sorry.

MAN: No, no. Shit by any other name would not smell as shit!

BOY: So, it was shit then?

MAN: As shit as it comes.

BOY: Good, because I thought I was missing something.

MAN: Nothing.

BOY: That's ok then.

Beat.

MAN: So?

BOY: So, when my friend copped off with some bit with glasses, I thought, I'd better split. But he said, 'No, be brave!' And he pointed at you and said 'Start there. That guy seems sussed.'

MAN: Sussed!

BOY: You know...

MAN: No one is sussed past forty!

BOY: Not sussed in that way... just, happy...

MAN: Oh, I'm over the moon!

BOY: You know what I mean.

MAN: You mean gay?

BOY: Just... sussed.

MAN: But I'm not gay, *per se*. I'm probably exactly like you. I've just gone past the questioning stage and now accept whatever comes. I think it's called, a slag!

BOY: Perhaps that's what I saw in you when I looked at you across the gallery...

MAN: The slag?

BOY: Something familiar.

Beat.

MAN: Oh. They say we search for our own reflections.

BOY: Yeah, I've heard that one.

MAN: Dorian Gray! In my mind I'm you, but are you me?

Beat.

BOY: What? Look, this is massive for me... sorry.

MAN: That's fine.

BOY: Just don't rush me. Ok?

MAN: 'An age at least to every part.'

BOY: Sorry?

MAN: I'll savour you like a childhood sweet sucked to death.

BOY: Another euphemism?

MAN: Metaphor. Everything sounds like an euphemism upon my lips. For sincerity, forget the words.

BOY: Will you kiss me?

MAN: Are you sure?

BOY: Yes.

MAN: If that's your desire?

BOY: Please.

They kiss.

MAN: Oh God.

BOY: What is it?

MAN: You'd better leave....

BOY: No.

MAN: Leave now, give us both a chance.

BOY: I don't want to go.

MAN: Please, you're too beautiful.

BOY: Is that a crime?

MAN: No, but it's been a long time since I even dared dream of beauty. I fear that if I reach out for beauty now, I'll kill it again.

BOY: You won't kill me. Please, I need this. I've nowhere else.

MAN: So I'm a last resort, am I?

BOY: You're a new beginning.

MAN: Have you closed the door?

BOY: Just you and me.

MAN: You'll kill me with beauty, I know you will.

BOY: Sure.

MAN (*thinks, to painting*): *My dear Butterfly, look at me. I'm aflame and he's dancing! My Little Moth!* Shit!

BOY: What's wrong?

MAN: It's embarassing, my condoms are two years out of date.

BOY: Don't worry. I went to the garage. (*He produces a pack from his trouser pocket.*)

MAN: Ah my Cupid, compromise me!

They entwine. After a while, MAN turns to painting.

MAN: Not here. (*He leads BOY off.*) Come....

Scene Three – The Betrayal

Boy enters, approaches the draped picture and uncovers it. Once again, the Butterfly picture is revealed. However, this time, Butterfly is within the composition. Suddenly, she animates, steps out of the canvas and in to the room.

GIRL: Debbie! Couldn't you think of a better name than Debbie?

BOY: It was the first name that came to me.

GIRL: Oh, I bet she came; your Anam Chara.

BOY: Please.

GIRL: Oozed like lava round your cock, did she?

BOY: Hello to you too!

GIRL: Synchronicity!

BOY: What?

GIRL: Isn't that what matters to you?

BOY: Sorry...

GIRL: Coming together!

BOY: Please...

GIRL: Well try synchronisation not 'icity' you dick! That's probably why you always had a problem with it. You should have checked the dictionary before fucking!

BOY: Look, if it still bugs you, the truth is, she never did.

GIRL: Never what?

BOY: She never came... ever, like that... together, you know. Only manually.

GIRL: Manually! What the hell was she? A Ford Mondeo!

BOY: You know what I mean!

GIRL: But still you fucked her... automatically, if nothing else! Let me say that again, you fucked her, you bastard! And when I was so fragile as well!

BOY: All right, I know.

GIRL: No, you could never know.

BOY: I tried to know.

GIRL: You didn't try hard enough. You cold shit.

BOY: I was cold! Shit, you were Ice Age!

GIRL: I was desperate.

BOY: You froze me out. I needed warmth.

GIRL: Didn't you think I needed warmth as well?

BOY: I couldn't have warmed you even if I'd poured petrol over our 'kiss' and lit a match.

GIRL: At least I would've known then that you cared! You've no idea; no idea how dead life can be. I'd wake in the morning cold with fear and as the day wore on, anxiety would just freeze me rigid... I was so fragile... so fragile; like a rose dipped in dry ice....

BOY: Do you think I didn't feel that? It's really hard moving around someone knowing she could shatter at any minute. So cold you'd say, so cold. I couldn't touch you without getting frostbitten.

GIRL: So you burnt your fingers on Debbie.

BOY: 'Us', was a dead loss. I felt useless.

GIRL: You felt useless!

BOY: So dark, you'd say. I tried for years to pull you into the sun, but you just went further into the shadows... away from me... away from yourself. So alone, you'd cry; I was lonely as well. I needed a life less fucking Arctic!

GIRL: And Debbie was tropical was she?

BOY: She was a freak warm day in October.

GIRL: Days!

BOY: All right! She was an Indian summer then. She came...

GIRL: Manually...

BOY: And went! No emotion, just warmth. But I was wrong. I know I was wrong, and I'm sorry.

GIRL: Really?

Pause.

BOY: I wanted you. I wanted the you I knew before you got ill, I wanted you badly but you'd gone; long before you disappeared.

GIRL: Well, I'm here now.

BOY: Yeah....

Pause.

GIRL: Dead but here.

Pause.

BOY : You beautiful shit... I've missed you.

GIRL: You took your time.

BOY: Time takes time.

GIRL: Oh, that's deep!

BOY: I felt guilty.

GIRL: I should think so.

BOY: I kept seeing you the last time you walked through the door; away from me; from yourself.

GIRL: I never walked away from myself, I knew I could never do that, but I walked away from you, no problem.

47

BOY: You know what I mean.

GIRL: Oh, I know what you mean. You came home that evening reeking of 'manual labour', which was odd because you worked at a desk! Humping filing cabinets, you said. Poor you. Humping filing cabinets! Tits! Can't be much fun, all that flesh on metal! Is that why you put Debbie in between you and the metal, to cushion the job? Bitch! I could smell her in your pants when you took them off; all musky, like our bed, but shittier.

BOY: You threw them at me in the bath?

GIRL: Did you expect me to wear them on my head and run through Clifton shouting, 'I am the Queen of Broken Hearts, pelt me with Tapas and bastard derision,' did you? Anyway, they needed a wash; brown tracks at the back, white at the front.

BOY: Please...

GIRL: You hurt me so deeply. I never thought you'd do that.

BOY: Yeah well... you were the one always accusing me of wanting other women.

GIRL: Turns out I was right in the end, doesn't it?

BOY: Self-fulfilling prophecy.

GIRL: Oh, here we go! My fault again!

BOY: You wanted to be right.

GIRL: Did I?

BOY: You wanted to be betrayed.

GIRL: Sure I did.

BOY: You had so little faith in yourself that you had no faith in me.

GIRL: Prosaic shit!

BOY: I loved you.

GIRL: How could you love me, then do what you did?

BOY: You were always down.

GIRL: Well, up's not a button you can press, ok. I was ill!

BOY: I know.... Fuck, I knew you were ill. That's why I panicked when you stormed out. I couldn't run after you, dripping wet. By the time I dressed you'd long gone. I tried everywhere; your friends, bars, cafes. No one had seen you.

GIRL: You should've tried Leigh Woods.

BOY: Leigh Woods?

GIRL: Yes.

BOY: Why there?

GIRL: Don't you remember? We went there for a walk when we first moved down from London.

BOY: Yeah, of course.

GIRL: We had no money, so we took sandwiches.

BOY: I remember.

GIRL: And where we sat down to eat them, in the hollow of a tree, was a pool. And floating on the surface of the water was a five pound note.

BOY: Sure.

GIRL: Put there for us by the fairies to wish us well in our new home, you said, and you made me come in the trees! Then we went to Clifton and bought coffee and cakes with the fiver. It was so warm in that cafe...

BOY: It was.

GIRL: So warm, it felt like home.

BOY: Mmm....

Pause.

GIRL: Well, I wanted warmth again, like you. I went looking for that tree, but I couldn't find it. I couldn't find it. I looked and looked. I was frantic with looking, but I couldn't find it... I couldn't find it. (*Almost crying.*) I've missed you, you shit.

BOY: And me, you.

GIRL: Missed, so much. I love you more than life.

BOY: You're dead!

GIRL: Shut up and just kiss me!

They kiss, passionately.

GIRL: So, tell me. What's it like to be kissed by a man?

BOY: Oh, come on.

GIRL: No, what was it like?

Beat.

BOY: All stubble!

GIRL: Now you know, moisturiser is not the devil's spunk!

BOY: I take it all back.

GIRL: Was it odd?

BOY: In what way?

GIRL: *Odd* odd?

BOY: No. It felt... sort of...

GIRL: Sort of what?

BOY: I don't know, sort of... knowing.

GIRL: Knowing!

BOY (*dismissively*): Oh, I don't know.

GIRL: You've just said you know.

BOY: Oh, come on...

GIRL: Well, I want to know.

BOY: Why?

GIRL: Because I've just listened to you two getting acquainted, I'm in no mood, so just tell me...

BOY: Ok, ok... it was... it was like...

GIRL: Like what!

BOY: I'm trying to find the words, all right! It's difficult. It's like, touching yourself. Yeah, touching yourself, but not.

GIRL: Oh! So what are you saying? Every gay act's a wank?

BOY: No, I'm not saying that. It just felt familiar, that's all.

GIRL: Familiar?

BOY: Yeah.

GIRL: How?

BOY: Like... oh, I don't know, like two football supporters who can name who scored where and when.

GIRL: That's a bit macho.

BOY: Yeah, well, gays like football as well, you know!

GIRL: Oh, sorry! One fuck and you're an expert on all things pink!

BOY : Why the shit did I bother coming here?

GIRL: To discover yourself, apparently!

BOY: Fuck off!

Pause.

GIRL: So was it disgusting?

BOY: Why should it be?

GIRL: Oh, of course. Why should it be, being the theoretical 'bi' you are?

BOY: I've always thought that there's no difference.

GIRL: In theory, yes, but in practice?

BOY: It was just a means to an end, nothing more. Isn't that why you fucked him?

GIRL: You bastard!

BOY : Well, isn't it?

Beat.

GIRL: Why I fucked him is my business. But you fucked him for me, so I have every right to know.

BOY (*deliberately*): Ok, if you want to know everything, it surprised me. Ok? Is that what you want to hear?

GIRL: Please...

BOY: I thought that was your fantasy, to see me with another man?

GIRL: I was alive then, nothing was real.

BOY: Well I'm alive now, and it was real to me.

GIRL: Bastard. If you were a woman, you'd be a slut!

BOY: I'll take that as a compliment.

GIRL: Take it and shove it up your newly-found hole!

BOY: Oh! Do you have to kill me, every time, do you? Is it not enough you killed yourself?

GIRL: You shit.

BOY: I'm only here for you. I only slept with him, for you. You asked for honesty, I'm just saying that it surprised me. Ok? So now you know

GIRL: Ok... but you're still a bastard.

BOY: That's me!

They laugh.

BOY: Come on, we're arguing like you never died! Sorry. Just tell me what happened after Leigh Woods.

GIRL: I don't know. I really don't know. I keep trying to see, but it's just mud to me. I guess I went to the Suspension Bridge but... but I can't see anything.

BOY: No?

GIRL: No.

BOYL Strange.

GIRL: Why?

BOY: Because I can see everything. I dream about it all the time. It haunts me. I can see you walk across the bridge, past the Samaritans sign that asks you to phone before you jump, but you don't. I'm hovering six feet above you like the fifth fucking province. I can see everything, but you don't see me. And I'm beside you as he helps you climb onto the rail.

GIRL: Was *he* there?

BOY: I can see him.

GIRL: Bastard!

BOY: People around you are stunned. It takes them a while to realise it's not a student prank or a cry for help. By then, a little push, and it's too late, you're flying; a little butterfly fragile in the wind hundreds of feet above the Avon; your wings iridescent in the summer sun. You fly through me, through my heart, down river. You follow the course of the Avon to the sea and aim for America. And as the sun dies, you drop down onto the golden swell to expire in the beauty of an ocean sunset. That's how I see it

GIRL: Then you see shit! I just slapped into the water; died before impact. I was washed down river to Portishead where a dog sniffed out my corpse in the mud!

BOY: Oh, thanks... thanks for destroying everything; thanks for every damn thing! (*He is angry.*)

GIRL: Oh... c'mon, don't be so down.

BOY: Me! Down? That's rich!

GIRL: Let's talk about something else. Talk about the City, where we met. Do you remember when we first saw each other?

He looks at her.

GIRL: The night of the postcard exhibition at the RA? Remember? And mine was hung next to the Grayson Perry. And within minutes there was a dot next to mine and I was thrilled.

BOY: He bought it, Mr fucking Critic...

GIRL: Yeah, but I didn't know that at the time, did I?

BOY: And what did he say to you when you found out?

GIRL: I forget.

BOY: I remember.

GIRL: You weren't even there!

BOY: 'You're a nobody,' he said. 'Nobody buys a nobody. But one day I'll make you a somebody, and then everybody'll want to buy you.' Twat!

56

GIRL: Ok... but at the time I thought a 'somebody' had bought me, and I was full of it.

BOY: Yeah, I know. I remember you walked across the bar towards our table; full of energy... more life in one person than I'd ever seen; like a black hole, you sucked me in, I'd head-fucked you before I realised it!

GIRL: What!

BOY: I can see you now, with your friends; all YBA wannabes, 'Saatchi' tattooed across your arses. Like Gods! You torched the room just by being in it. I loved you from the moment you scorched me and left me for ash on the floor.

GIRL: I was with him at the time; time wasn't right.

BOY: No, you had a career to think about, so you went home to fuck a corpse when you could've made love to the living.

GIRL: Oh, come on...

BOY: How could you love that shell?

GIRL: He wasn't a shell then, I loved him. (*She looks daggers.*) Why do I always have to justify? I loved him. Ok?

BOY: More than you love me?

GIRL: I left him for you, didn't I!

BOY: Eventually!

GIRL: I lost everything for you. No, nearly everything. I lost everything when you fucked Debbie!

BOY: How many times can I say sorry?

GIRL: Not enough!

BOY: I'll say it all you want. I'm sorry, I'm sorry...

GIRL: I don't want you to say it, I want you to mean it.

BOY: I do mean it. Honestly, I do.

GIRL: Yeah...

Pause.

BOY: How did you meet him, anyway?

GIRL: Does it matter?

BOY: Yeah.

GIRL: How did you meet Debbie?

BOY: I worked with her.

GIRL: How convenient!

BOY: And him?

GIRL: I've told you before.

BOY: No, you haven't, actually.

GIRL: I know I have.

BOY: No you haven't. So tell me now. I want to know, before I kill him.

GIRL: Sh...

BOY: He's dead to the world, he can't hear a thing. How did you meet him?

GIRL: He... if you must know, he came to a group exhibition just off Tower Bridge. Friends of mine had asked me to contribute and um... well, I'd seen him before; openings, galleries, stuff.... I knew who he was. He was younger then, not like now. He was... vital, and I was...

BOY: Cock happy...

GIRL: Flattered. I saw him a few times, then he asked me to move in...

BOY: And you got your gallery and good reviews with one stone!

GIRL (*reluctantly*): Yeah.

BOY: What's the casting couch for artists? The exhibition easel!

GIRL: Do you have to!

BOY: Did you?

GIRL (*staring, coldly*): Grow up, will you! I met people with him I wouldn't have met otherwise; doors opened, what's wrong with that? That's what it's all about; knowing and being known, Jopling on your mobile phone, a fag shared with Lucas at the Chapman brothers' opening. I mean, no one wants to be a sad fuck like Gwen John?

BOY: I thought she met all the right people!

GIRL: Not in the right context... not in the right time! I was a twentieth-century girl! I didn't need a Rodin, I needed an Appolinaire!

BOY: Art is sick.

GIRL: Life is sick! You know, I haven't told you this before, and I know I haven't told you, because it would've totally fucked you off on your four-eighty an hour at the call centre. You thought I stole our Gwen John, didn't you? Took it from his wall as payment for being fucked! Well the truth is, I didn't, I bought it in Cork Street the day my grant cheque cleared. It was the price of a whole term's grant, but I bought it. That's the beauty of being kept, no responsibility!

I was well chuffed, I owned a piece of brilliance and I hoped that it would rub off on me. He asked me where I'd bought it. 'Oh, yeah!' he said, giving away nothing. He said nothing for months. Then the first time he suspected 'us', he went ape. And we were arguing, really arguing like father and kid! And he shouted, 'You're like a child!' And I shouted, 'I am one, and you're a fucking granddad!' 'Fuck you!' he said. 'And one more thing, your Gwen John's a fake!' And I screamed, 'Bollocks, you prick', and he shouted, 'No, my little cunt. Wrong paper, wrong line and she never signed; too self-effacing, not like you. Game set and fucking match!'

He slapped me down! Smug fuck; all age and knowledge. I was so mad; I didn't want to believe him, but I needed to find out. A few weeks after that, I took a train to Cardiff where this expert proved him right. Empty, dead bastard! A dream destroyer, that's all he is!

Beat.

BOY: Don't worry. He's going to pay with whatever life he's got left in him. I saw you die because of him. And you may be beyond that pain, but I'm not. He fucked me long before tonight, tonight was just the act.

GIRL: Oh, my brave Orpheus.

BOY: I'm here for us.

GIRL (*considering*): Just, turn 'round, don't look back. Walk through the door and live for us both.

BOY: No, I've come too far for that.

Pause.

GIRL: Then make love to me, before he wakes. Lie with me, in the shame he covers me with, and fuck me to death.

BOY: I'll warm you to life.

GIRL: You can try...

BOY: I hate him....

They kiss and lie in the canvas which used to hide her portrait. Eventually, they entwine within it.

61

GIRL: Sh. if you kill him, kill him coldly... the way he killed me!

BOY: I will.

GIRL: Do you remember after I walked out on him to be with you? Do you remember the first thing he did, do you remember? He had a word with my gallery.

BOY: Yeah.

GIRL: And the bastards dumped me because of him.

BOY: I know.

GIRL: Fucked his Pygmalion big-time! Quiet words and screaming fucking reviews... trashing me in journals; really bad mentions in 'Contemporary' and 'Frieze'... personal stuff...

BOY: It doesn't matter.

GIRL: It matters to me, Bill. I was rejected; a Rousseau in my own time – ridiculed; I felt so alone. How can you be that lonely in a city? No exhibitions, no commissions, nothing. He killed my future, Bill... fucked me.

BOY: He fucked us both.

GIRL: He left me with nothing.

BOY: You had me.

GIRL: Oh, I know, I know I had you. But the more you loved me, the further away I drifted from my own heart....

In the end, I was barely a pulse.... I should've loved you more than anything, but I couldn't. I was too weak. So angry with the world, with myself, not strong enough.

BOY: Sh... sh...

GIRL: I was gifted, wasn't I; a part of the zeitgeist?

BOY: You were.

GIRL: So why were doors slammed in my face; roads crossed to avoid me, as if I'd killed Saatchi and burnt the fucking meal ticket? Bastards! He had no right to do that just because I didn't want to fuck him any more. Things change.

BOY: That's why I thought it was best for us to get out.

GIRL: I know, and I love you for caring. And Bristol's a beautiful city, but it's not London is it? it's not even Cardiff. At least Cardiff has a nation to paint! Bristol has nothing but black blood and the Primrose Cafe; dead white city! In London, you said I burnt with life. In Bristol, I was a dying ember choking for air; if it's sad to see a flame die, it kills to feel the flame die in your own heart.

BOY: It's why I came looking for you.

GIRL: Five years in 2D... so cold. Re-animate me, inflame me.

BOY: I will... I will...

GIRL: Do you still love me, Bill?

BOY: Of course.

GIRL: Will you ever stop loving me?

BOY: I would die for you.

GIRL: My sweet, sweet William.

They make love beneath the canvas.

Scene Four – The Revenge

MAN stirs from sleep and walks on.

MAN: Moth! My Little Moth! Are you there, dear Moth? My beautiful... (*he sees the canvas has been taken from the painting – his tone changes*) prick of a Moth! I'll torch you, you filching shit! Butterfly! My beautiful Butterfly. What has he done with you? Where has he taken you? By now, you're probably underground in the Ukraine where stolen Munchs scream. Bastard! I thought his accent was odd; round and about, my arse! Bloody Russian mafia; delicatessens on every fucking corner!

At least you're not bronze, worth 'Moore' to a philistine as scrap! There again, perhaps you've been stolen to order? But who would want you? Everyone who's looked at you, that's who! Who was at the funeral... all the exhibitions? Think! I'll steal the remark books, check addresses! The little git's studied you. He'll fall in love with you, even if he hasn't yet, he will, and you with him; sodding Stockholm syndrome! Last time I waste Montrachet on a shit! Next fuck gets Liebfraumilch!

Wait wait wait, I'm missing something here. His wings! (*He sees BOY's clothes.*) You're still here, aren't you, my little graduate! I've caught you inflagrante... how delicious! Well, I'm no hero, but it's either over my dead body or yours. And believe you me, I'll gladly skewer you like a pole up Frida Khalo's crack for the sake of my Butterfly! (*He's unsure.*) So, *veni veni* Mephistopheles! Reveal yourself, you dun-coloured shit!

BOY reveals himself, from beneath the canvas.

MAN: *Ecce* fucking *Homo*! Where's Butterfly, you bastard? What have you done with her?

BOY: She's here.

MAN: Where?

GIRL is revealed from beneath the canvas, but MAN cannot see her.

BOY: Here.

MAN: Don't play the fool with me!

BOY: I'm not.

MAN: You want a conflict to resolve? Resolve this one!

BOY: Look...

MAN: I'd like to look, so tell me!

BOY: She's here.

MAN: Where? Where!

BOY and GIRL realise MAN cannot see her. MAN goes for the corkscrew.

GIRL: He can't see me.

MAN: You may have twenty years on me...

GIRL: Twenty-five.

MAN: But I'm the man packing the corkscrew, and either you tell me, or this point is your pin! *Capiche?*

GIRL: Careful, he's fifty and desperate!

MAN: I'm not talking Poussin here; no fucking allegory.

BOY: What should I do?

MAN: Just tell me!

GIRL: Tell him I'm flying around the room.

MAN: I'm waiting.

BOY: What?

MAN: My patience is veneer!

GIRL: Tell him that.

BOY: Ok (*In fear, as MAN approaches.*) She's flying around the room.

GIRL sings.

MAN: Do you take me for a fool? She wouldn't fly for you! You can fuck me, but don't bluff me!

GIRL: Buy time.

BOY: What?

MAN: What!

GIRL: Tell him you can see me.

BOY: I'm sorry!

MAN: Too late!

GIRL: Just tell him you can see me!

MAN: I'm going to pin you fucking rigid, Moth!

Beat.

BOY: I can see her!

MAN: What?

BOY: I can see her.

MAN (*thinks, then*): Don't shit lies on me.

BOY: No lies.

MAN: Then prove it.

BOY: How?

MAN: How does she fly?

BOY: How? She flies... like this.... (*He uses his arms as wings.*)

MAN (*astonished at BOY's stupidity, and dismissive*): You'd be too-bastard-grotesque for Bosch!

GIRL: Tell him 'I fly in grace'.

BOY: She flies...

MAN: Yes, but how?

BOY: In grace....

MAN: In grace?

GIRL: And beauty.

BOY: And beauty. She flies in grace and beauty!

MAN: What?

BOY: She flies in grace and beauty.

Pause.

MAN: Grace and beauty! (*The words hit him like a stone.*) You can see her?

BOY: Yes.

MAN: If you can see her, where is she now?

BOY: In front of you.

MAN: Where?

GIRL lightly strokes MAN's cheek.

BOY: Did you feel that?

MAN: Yes.

BOY: That was her wing brushing your cheek.

MAN: Her wing? Oh my Butterfly, brush me again... please my beauty? I'll turn the other cheek...

GIRL (*hissing, near MAN's face*): But I won't, you bastard!

BOY: Did you feel that breath upon your face.

MAN: Yes.

BOY: That was her kiss.

MAN: I felt that, but I still can't see her. I can't see you, my dead beauty. I've seen no beauty in the world since you left me; all is ugly... so ugly; shit state of affairs for a critic! I know it's partly my fault. I shouldn't have destroyed you in the way I did, but age distorts, my beauty. You can't mess with the over-forty, our skins are thinner and less elastic. Can you forgive me?

GIRL: See the shit I've had to endure!

BOY: She says no.

MAN: You can hear her as well?

GIRL: No-o!

Half-pause.

BOY: Yes.

MAN (*thinks, then*): Look, whatever's happened between us tonight, has happened; best forgotten in cups, agreed? So tell me, hand on heart. Can you really hear her?

BOY: Yes.

MAN: Really. Now, not that I don't trust you, I just want... an assurance, you understand. Thomas by name, Thomas by nature.

BOY: Sure.

MAN: So humour me, ok? I'd like to ask her a question. If that's ok with you? Just one question, her answer'll be proof enough that it's really her.

BOY: But you don't need to ask through me. She can hear you. Ask her yourself.

MAN: You mean now?

BOY: She has always heard you.

MAN: Always?

GIRL: Ad nauseam.

BOY: Yes.

MAN: Oh, my God. Well if you can hear me, my beauty, answer this, just so that I know it's you and not this blithe spirit fucking with me! Which artist do I most admire?

GIRL: Piss easy.

BOY: Too easy.

MAN: Oh?

GIRL: I'd like to flatter myself and think it's me, but I know it's not. You fucked me but never admired me, you bastard....

Pause.

MAN: Well?

GIRL: Don't tell him that.

MAN: Still guessing? That easy! You're lying, aren't you?

GIRL: It's Caravaggio.

BOY: Caravaggio.

MAN: Caravaggio... clever. Was it the lizards? Was it?

MAN looks at BOY. BOY is confused.

MAN: No. But why? Tell me why.

GIRL (*quickly, in anger*): Because, like him, you claim to have no venial sins, only mortal ones... that's you and me, Bill. Like Caravaggio, you love both youths and prostitutes, but in place of the artist's sword you carry your pen – much more killing! Your favourite pictures are of his bare shouldered boys, though lately you prefer the darker pictures of the artist in exile. In particular, Salome with the head of John the Baptist, because you are also a twat betrayed, and like Caravaggio, you have killed, and as a consequence, an exile in your own fucking self! And soon, you will also die an untimely death as he did. Tell him that.

BOY: All of it?

MAN: All of what?

BOY: Nothing.

MAN: After five years, each syllable, each breath is a big something. So tell me everything.

BOY: She just said... well, she's sort of disappointed because she would've liked to have flattered herself by thinking that she was the artist you most admired in the world, or words to that effect...

MAN: Oh, my poor love...

GIRL: Why the hell did you tell him that?

MAN: My Butterfly, please forgive me, I said admire, not love. I love you above all. I admire Caravaggio as one admires Mozart, but loves Mantovani.

GIRL: What!

MAN: I have always loved your vision and integrity, you know that. From that first moment sketching butterflies in the Saatchi. Even when you hitched up with that bastard who took you off to rot in the provinces; Bangor, Bognor, some buggering place! Had you lived, a year or two in obscurity, just outside the M25 perhaps, then I would've rekindled your career; even if you hadn't come back to me, I would have championed you, made you flame again. I just needed time... I was hurt. Rejection is mortifying at my age. With time you'll grow to realise that... no, I guess you won't, will you. Look... (*to BOY*) is she still listening?

BOY: Yes.

MAN: Where is she?

BOY: In front of you.

GIRL stands beside BOY.

MAN: Ok, what I have to say is personal. So, if you wouldn't mind just staying back. Just be my ears.

BOY: If you say.

MAN (*speaking tenderly*): Give me her responses, verbatim, ok. I'd just appreciate a bit of distance. But remember, each breath, each nuance...

BOY: Sure.

MAN: Thank you. (*He goes down stage and confesses.*)

MAN: My dear Butterfly, no big words, no shit, as you would say, just as it is... or as it was.

GIRL: Oh, God...

MAN: I'd never given anything of myself to anybody before giving my heart to you, you know that. I knew, that day, when I looked at you sketching butterflies, that I would give my life to you... for you; all that I'd held back from others who demanded so much from me, but received so little. Even had I never seen you again, you would have been my Beatrice and I would have loved you to the grave and beyond.

Anyway, I felt so gauche asking you to dinner that first night. The cynic in me knew that to accept was a career move on your behalf, possibly. I just hoped that attraction played some small part in your decision to grace me with your beauty. I felt truly blessed the night we dined... it was divine. Some weeks later when you agreed to move in, I almost turned Christian! Then when you turned up with your bags and canvases, I saw the light and partook of the body and drank the blood... along with a very good cheese, as I recall!

So hopeful. You filled me with hope; the hope the years had slowly drained away. But you replenished me with enthusiasm, idealism, conceptualism, all the god-damn 'isms'! After being so cold for so long, I warmed to life again, dancing around your incandescent beauty.

Pause.

MAN: But ours was to be only a brief moment in the sun, wasn't it? Before the clouds covered again and the cold returned. It wasn't your affair with Bill that chilled me. By then I had already began to freeze! What dropped me to absolute bloody zero...

GIRL: Tell him to stop!

MAN: Was your decision to...

BOY: Will you stop?

MAN: Sorry?

BOY: She asks you to stop?

MAN: No.

GIRL: Please, you bastard!

BOY: She says please!

MAN: No! She will listen to me because she owes it to me to do so! (*To GIRL.*) You owe a life, so listen for a few brief moments of your eternal death, my dear Buttterfly!

GIRL: I'm sorry, Bill.

BOY: What for?

GIRL: Just sorry, ok.

BOY: Why?

MAN: I'll give her 'what for' and fucking 'why!'

GIRL (*puts her hands over her ears*): La la la la. I am not listening to you. I am not listening to you.

MAN: What froze me to death was her decision to rob us both of the only true warmth we would ever find. When she, when you...

GIRL: Don't...

MAN: When you terminated your pregnancy. When you did that, all hope was killed in us both...

GIRL: No!

MAN: I would've married you, Butterfly, renegotiated my life...

GIRL: I didn't want your life!

MAN: I wanted our child desperately, if only to prove that there could be a purpose to the life of an ageing critic. The vacuousness of opinion, the waste of words... so much 'tapioca de fucking wankeur' spilt in vain! I should've been consumed at birth by rabid dogs! Eaten before my first howl! O... o... o... o...

GIRL sings.

MAN: That's why the simple promise of good coming out of me, out of us both, filled me with the joy of a life lived a little less in vain. For the first time in this pathetic existence, I was happy knowing that I had helped create an unspoken statement that could never be reviewed. I just didn't expect, I really didn't expect the critic in you to review your own fucking work so harshly!

GIRL: Bastard!

MAN: I loved you, my Butterfly. I loved the promise created between us as much as I hated its destruction; I know your body's your own, but for a brief period, it carried a part of me, a part, I hoped, would grow into the most sublime piece of work.

BOY (*to GIRL*): You never told me this!

MAN: It doesn't concern you. Just tell me what she says?

BOY: Sorry?

MAN: What is she saying?

BOY: She's singing.

MAN: A sad song?

BOY: An empty one.

MAN: Oh, my dead beauty. After you left, I spiralled into darkness, down to a depth from which, I believed, I would never surface. I know I took you down with me and left you for dead, I'm sorry... *peccavi*, my love, *peccavi*, but I was so hurt. I hate what I did, I hated it at the time of doing it, and if I had a soul it would be yours, but I don't, I have only words.

GIRL: Too many fucking words!

MAN: Dear Butterfly, I know you had your reasons; only twenty-one, ambition, and you probably didn't want to walk into Parentcraft with your grandfather on your arm! Ok, it saddens me, but I can accept that, because I love you and I can't stop loving you, and the deeper the loss, the deeper I love.

GIRL: You shallow shit!

MAN: We both made mistakes. All I ask is that you forgive me, as I forgive you. Please?

GIRL: I have done nothing to forgive!

BOY: She says no.

MAN: Is that her answer?

GIRL: And don't remind me of our loss!

BOY: Yeah.

MAN: My beauty.

GIRL: Our loss, my arse! I was the one who lived and died with it. You only played with the idea of it. You didn't lie there and regret a moment too late. You weren't the one that was told you've blown your only chance of a child. We're sorry, but from now on, you'll create nothing but canvases! You have no idea how killing that can be – your razor criticism; fucking scything! Then five years hanging like a Renaissance nude behind drapes in the Vatican, watching you pull your pants down long after you've pissed yourself! You killed whatever pity I had left in me to hate you with. You leave me cold!

MAN: What is she saying?

BOY: Still singing.

MAN: Singing what?

BOY: A fuck-off song.

MAN: So I've just pissed down a Duchamp have I? Heartless bitch! Well, If that's the way it is, it's Bill I feel sorry for! Did you ever tell him the truth? Did you, my

Butterfly? Did you ever tell him why you could never have children because of the complications after the abortion? Did you tell him that?

GIRL: Bastard!

BOY: Serious?

MAN: Oh, I felt that breath! And did you blame me for everything? Did you? Did you play the little victim? Truth is, you were never my victim. I was yours; a willing victim, but a victim all the same! Is she still listening?

BOY: We were both victims.

MAN: Both?

BOY: Both her and me!

MAN: What?

BOY: Butterfly and Moth.

MAN: What are you on about?

BOY: Us.

MAN: You?

BOY: Me!

Beat of realisation.

MAN: Oh, my God...

BOY (*sings*): There were two in the bed and the little one said, roll over, roll over...

MAN (*for whom the penny drops*): Bill?

BOY: On the nail!

MAN: But what about your girlfriend's brother and the bathroom wank?

BOY: Butterfly was an only child, remember.

MAN: Yes, but...

BOY (*knowingly*): No but.

Beat.

MAN: You've been lying all night?

BOY: More or less.

Beat.

MAN: And were you a virgin?

BOY: Don't!

MAN: Verging on the fucking ridiculous, more like it! Bastard! And Butterfly?

BOY: She's no lie. She's here. She's heard everything.

MAN: She's hearing this?

BOY: Yes, and loving it.

Pause.

MAN: Why are you here, Bill?

BOY: I could say synchronicity, but, being honest, it's just simple revenge.

MAN: Why?

BOY: For killing beauty. Why do you think?

MAN: Bill, she killed herself.

BOY: Says who?

MAN: The inquest. The verdict was suicide.

BOY: Lies.

MAN: She jumped from Bristol Suspension Bridge!

BOY: Yes, but who helped her jump?

MAN: Who?

BOY: Who pushed her?

MAN: Are you serious!

BOY: I saw you.

MAN: C'mon, Bill, please. The moment she jumped, I was sweating in the Arsenale in Venice.

BOY: I don't give a shit whether you were sweating from your arse in fucking Torquay!

MAN: What!

BOY: You were there, egging her on. I saw you as I hovered above her but could do nothing to save her. You helped her onto the rail, you told her she could fly, then pushed her.

MAN: For God's sake!

BOY: Don't! Don't you dare! We're both bored shitless with your fucking lies and your arty-farty wank!

MAN: Look, I think I'd better call someone...

BOY: No calls! This is just between us three; you, me and Butterfly. We both think it's time you realised the pain your words inflict. Did you really think you could destroy without effect? Did you? What did you read in Poly?

MAN: Humanities.

BOY: You should've read science; cause and effect, mate! All those bad words, all that bitterness... never lost, it just goes around...

MAN: Please, Bill.

BOY: Way too late for a please. You see, you are the conflict, and I'm resolving it!

MAN: Look, Bradford, love it! And I'll pay whatever you want.

BOY: Why are you always so sarky? You went to the Poly not the bastard Uni! And it's not about the money, it's about the art; her world; her heaven. The heaven you made hell. You admitted that, I heard you tell her as much.

MAN: That was a private conversation.

BOY: A bit one-sided for a conversation, wasn't it?

MAN: What?

BOY: She said things.

MAN: What things?

BOY: Things you didn't hear. Bad things, very bad things about you... I spared you the worst. You should thank me.

MAN (*to himself*): Oh, my beauty...

Beat.

BOY: She hates you; the depths you dragged her down to, the despair... a deep loathing. But she doesn't loathe alone, because I got dragged down as well, didn't I. And it was so dark and cold, and I was there one hell of a long time, 'suffering is one fuck of a long moment!' All your fault, your fucking fault and you've admitted it.

MAN: I was speaking metaphorically. You don't know the context.

BOY: Oh, I know the context, you twat! I was the one who nursed her through all the pain; all the despair you caused her with your cutting criticism; very fucking Oxford! Words so sharp they fucking sliced, then stripped her bare until there was nothing left but bone.

MAN: Just words, Bill; my vocation...

BOY: Over and above the call of duty, mate; too personal and vindictive by half! So, it's payback time. I am the fucking invoice! Bill by name, Bill by nature. Butterfly has asked me to take revenge... coldly, as you killed her.

MAN: Please...

GIRL: Just kill him.

BOY: Did you hear that? Just kill him, she said. She's very angry, very angry with you. Her patience is... (*knowingly*) Vermeer.

MAN: Veneer.

BOY: I know what I said. It was *une plaisanterie*! I was trying to lighten the situation!

MAN: It's very funny.

BOY: Butterfly laughed. Didn't you?

BOY approaches MAN, threateningly.

BOY: So it seems that I'm packing the corkscrew this time, so you *capiche* me. What was that wine called in the seventies? Bull's Blood? Bullshit or something? You should know, being a connoisseur of fine wine and words.

MAN: Bull's Blood.

BOY: Bullshit! And tonight I think I'll open a bottle. Butterfly would like a glass. Wouldn't you. And I've always preferred red, as you know. So, open your shirt.

MAN: What?

BOY: Well I don't want to stain it, do I? Looks Jermyn Street to me.

MAN: It's Marks and Spencer's.

BOY grabs MAN and pins him down.

BOY: Oh. Fuck it then!

BOY rips open MAN's shirt.

MAN: Please, Bill, please don't do this!

BOY: Be a man, not a fucking critic!

MAN: For God's sake.

BOY: You don't believe in God! And anyway, he's not fucking listening!

MAN: My Butterfly, forgive me, forgive me, please.

BOY: I told you, don't beg, you fuck! It's ugly, past forty!

MAN: Oh, fuck.. fuck off... just fuck off... please fuck off, please... ah...

BOY jabs corkscrew into MAN's heart. Blood flows from both the wound and MAN's mouth. As it does, BOY collects it in a wine glass.

MAN: My Butterfly... beauty...

BOY: Beauty! She hit the mud and bloated on the tide. Then drifted down stream to rest in the sand like a wreck. Seagulls pecked at her eyes as she lay there... ugly. She should've danced in grace; danced in grace, touched the divine. But she didn't. Because of you! But you're free from him now, my Butterfly! Fly!

BOY drinks. GIRL sings.

The following two speeches can dovetail:

BOY: I've been thinking I'll organise a retrospective. Main galleries this time. Not Croydon; my mistake, sorry! You've been in the dark too long, the light'll do you good. What do you say, my beauty? Butterfly? Butterfly? You hiding from me? I can't see you anymore? So quiet, I can't hear you sing... Butterfly... are you there? Don't leave me... not after I've waited so long to see you again. I couldn't cope with loosing you a second time. Beauty... it's getting dark... cold.

A million butterflies fill the room.

MAN: I can you see you... see you... Butterfly... wings... sun... beautiful, beautiful love... your song... smell... dew on wings. Oh, I can feel... your kiss... my cheek. Land on my tongue... (*in agony and ecstasy*) there... taste fear. Sh, sh... no lizards... in my wine... no more, reviews... no... no more... words....

Pause.

BOY: My butterfly?

MAN: Just beauty...

GIRL sings as she soars....

PARTHIAN

diverse probing
profound
epic comic
urban
rural savage
new
writing

www.inpressbook s.co.uk

Llyfrau ar-lein
Books on-line